Mrs. Simms

The Snarth Goes to School

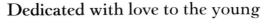

Dedicated with love to the young
Snarths in the family—
Daniel Stephen Hart,
Christina Marie Hart,
and Frank Louis Sergi
…and to Suzanne Sorice, with gratitude.
—Tessa & Frank

For Margaret, Emily and Kimba.
Thank you for your never-ending patience.
—Pietri Freeman

Book and cover design: schererMedia

Printed in Mexico

Hart, Tessa.
    The Snarth goes to school / by Tessa Hart and
Frank Sergi ; illustrated by Pietri Freeman —
1st ed.
    p. cm.
    LCCN: 99-76582
    ISBN: 0-9660172-0-X
    SUMMARY: The Snarth is a flamboyant creature who has been around for a long time and has made many friends throughout history. It has adopted Katrina Mann's family, but trouble starts when it wants to attend school with her.

    1. Animals, Mythical — Juvenile fiction.
    2. Elementary schools — Juvenile fiction.
    3. Toleration — Juvenile fiction.   I. Sergi, Frank.
    II. Freeman, Pietri.   III. Title.

PZ7.H2576Sn 2000   [Fic]
                          QBI99-1877

The Snarth
Goes to School

BY TESSA HART & FRANK SERGI

ILLUSTRATED BY PIETRI FREEMAN

ATRINA MANN stared at her oatmeal and orange juice and silently ordered her stomach to calm down! A bunch of butterflies were banging around down there, mixed with a million Mexican jumping beans. It was silly to be so nervous! So what if it was the first day of her second week in a new school…and so what if she was small for her age, and had never gone to a new school before? She would make friends there. Of course she would! Even if there was this one thing about her family that was sort of…hard to explain.

Her eyes slid up to the creature sitting across from her, and she couldn't help smiling. There was the Snarth slurping up breakfast without a care in the world, busily vacuuming Cheerios and corn dogs into its long flexible lips. Its delicate fingers waved in rhythm as it hummed a happy tune. The Snarth had lived with the Manns as long as Katrina could remember, and it always hummed exactly the same tune. But somehow, no one ever got tired of hearing it.

The Snarth's lips glowed a contented pinkish-green under the kitchen light. It caught Katrina's eye and cheerfully said, "Beep!"

"Beep, yourself, Snarth!" replied Katrina. She picked up her spoon.

At the other end of the table sat Katrina's parents, who had been watching her pick at her breakfast. They always knew when she was upset.

"Honey, do you want to tell us more about your new school?" asked her mom. "How do you like your teacher?"

Katrina took a deep breath. "It's okay, I guess, Mom. We have lots of kids in our class…almost every seat is full. The other kids have been going there since first grade…I ate lunch by myself on Friday." Katrina saw her parents looking at each other. She tried to think of some good things to say. "Mrs. Callahan is pretty nice. We're learning about Cleopatra and the pyramids, and in science we're going to study dinosaurs, and there's going to be a Science Fair…."

The Snarth had stopped eating. Its lips drooped like melting rubber toward its plate. Its hair, which normally stood up like bright yellow corn-stalks, now wilted dejectedly on its spindly neck. Then it let out a long, flubbery sigh. Katrina knew what was coming next.

"I want to go to school, too!" blubbered the Snarth in its wet, squeaky voice. "I want to carry a lunch box and ride on the bus!"

Katrina shuddered as she remembered the lunch box the Snarth had wanted to buy at the Dime-O-Mart. Orange plaid, purple polka dots and neon yellow squiggles all jumbled together! She said, for about the millionth time, "You can't go to school, Snarth. School is for kids, and you're not exactly a kid. Anyhow, remember what happened last year?"

The Snarth had snuck into her second grade classroom just one time, and the janitor was probably still trying to clean up all the glitter, confetti and lip-slime.

The Snarth hung its head and let out a tiny sob. Katrina could have kicked herself.

"I'm sorry, Snarth," she said gently. "But besides, they make you do all kinds of stuff in school that you wouldn't want to do. Like drink milk, and sit still. And they don't even have corn dogs in the cafeteria."

By this time the Snarth's lips were slumped across the table.

"Poor Snarth," said Mrs. Mann in a soothing voice. Katrina knew it broke her mother's heart to see the Snarth so sad. "But you have so many other fun things to do, dear. Why, you could make a fort out of all those branches that fell during the storm, and invite some squirrels to come over and play Capture the Flag."

"But I want to go to school," insisted the Snarth.

"Or you could get some tadpoles out of the creek and teach them synchronized swimming, just like last year," continued Mrs. Mann.

"BUT I WANNA GO TO SCHOOL!" bleated the Snarth.

Katrina sighed. Why couldn't she and the Snarth just trade places?

Mr. Mann cleared his throat. Everyone fell silent.

"You can't go to school, Snarth, and that's that," he pronounced. "I'm late for work, and Katrina, you have a school bus to catch." He folded the newspaper and rose from the table. Breakfast was over.

An hour later, Katrina was sitting in her class at Cedarville Elementary listening as Mrs. Callahan talked about ancient Egypt. A sunbeam fell across Katrina's desk and touched her face. Her eyes closed. She saw herself in a white robe in the hot sun of the desert — Katrina, Queen of the Nile.

All at once she heard a loud "THUNK!" as though a wet, slimy rubber plunger had attached itself to the window. No…it couldn't be! she thought as she peeked through her eyelashes. But sure enough, there was the Snarth, staring into the classroom with its lips glued to the window. Katrina groaned.

The next thing she knew, the Snarth was sitting next to her where Zoe Greenberg would've been if she hadn't caught the flu. The Snarth was only a little more than three feet tall, so its head barely cleared the desk, and only the tips of its long feet touched the floor. "Snarth, go home!" hissed Katrina under her breath. But the Snarth didn't even hear her. It was leaning forward, lips quivering, hanging on Mrs. Callahan's every word with a look of pure joy. Katrina hadn't seen the Snarth so happy since the day it had discovered miniature powdered doughnuts.

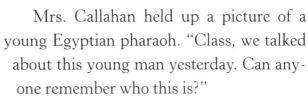

Mrs. Callahan held up a picture of a young Egyptian pharaoh. "Class, we talked about this young man yesterday. Can anyone remember who this is?"

Katrina reached over to plug the Snarth's lips, but it was too late. Without even raising its hand the Snarth blurted out, "That's King Tut! He was my friend. He was just a boy when they made him king. He got to stay up as late as he wanted. Sometimes we played Chinese checkers and ate papyrus dogs all night!"

Katrina groaned again. The kids in front of her were turning around, trying to see who was talking in that squeaky voice. Mrs. Callahan smiled, but looked puzzled. Did she have another new pupil in her class?

As Mrs. Callahan came closer, the Snarth looked up alertly into her face with the sweetest, most innocent expression she had ever seen. But for that matter, she had never seen an orangey-pink third grader with long tubular lips, spiky yellow hair, a pot belly with a light dusting of fur, and big, flat feet shaped like paddles. "Who are you?" she asked.

Before the Snarth could say anything Katrina stood up nervously and said, in her politest talk-to-the-teacher voice, "Ma'am, that's the Snarth. It lives in my house."

"Oh?" said Mrs. Callahan, looking as though she wanted to ask a few more questions. But just then the bell rang and everyone ran outside for recess. The Snarth darted out the door with Katrina at its heels.

The Snarth had the time of its life at recess! It turned its lips into a see-saw for the smaller children. It sucked up balls that ended up on the roof or down the gutter. It nuzzled Marcus Wilson's skinned knee with cool, soothing lip-slime. It beeped delightedly as it danced itself into a tornado to entertain everyone. Katrina began to enjoy recess, too. In fact, some of the kids in her class asked her to play with them because they thought she had brought the Snarth to school! She watched as the happy Snarth leaped all around the school yard—up and down and up and…

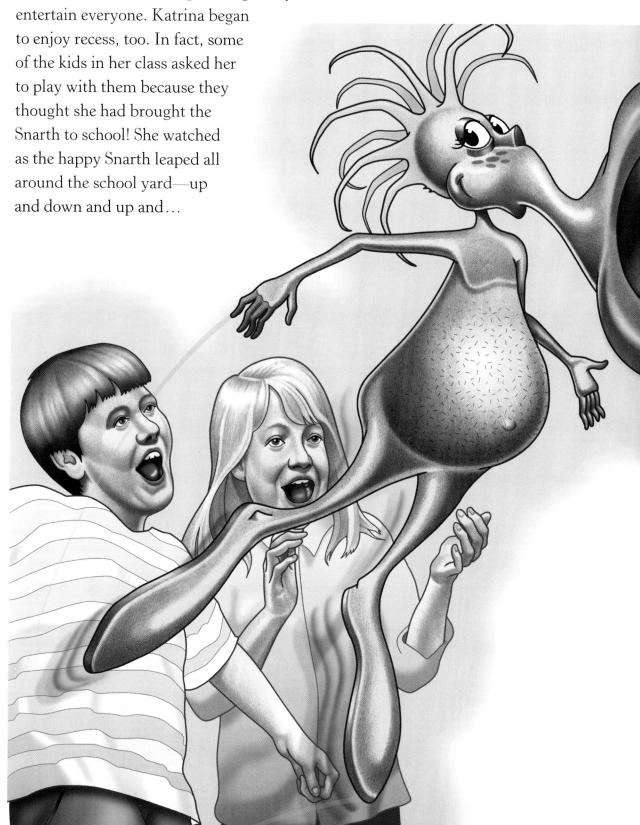

 —right into the
arms of Mr. Flatt,
the stubby, flat-
headed school principal who always looked mad.

"What the—" sputtered Mr. Flatt. The Snarth responded by
cheerfully flapping its lips back and forth across the principal's face.

"Oh, no!" whispered Katrina. That crazy Snarth was flubbering
Mr. Flatt!

Mr. Flatt was streaked with lip-slime. He looked as though he had
been attacked by a huge piece of wet taffy.

Katrina rushed over to pull the Snarth off Mr. Flatt. "Snarth," she
cried, "Say you're sorry, and let's get out of here!"

"Does this—this—THING belong to you, young lady?" demanded
Mr. Flatt, vainly trying to brush the sticky threads off his tie. It was worse
than rubber cement.

Katrina hesitated. "Why yes, I guess it does, in a way, Sir," she
admitted. She looked down at the Snarth, who was nodding vigorously.

"Well, then, get it away from this school yard NOW. And keep
it away!"

"NO!" shrieked the Snarth. "Please let me stay. Please, please—
I love it here!" And it dissolved into passionate tears.

Mr. Flatt gave Katrina a menacing look and stormed off.

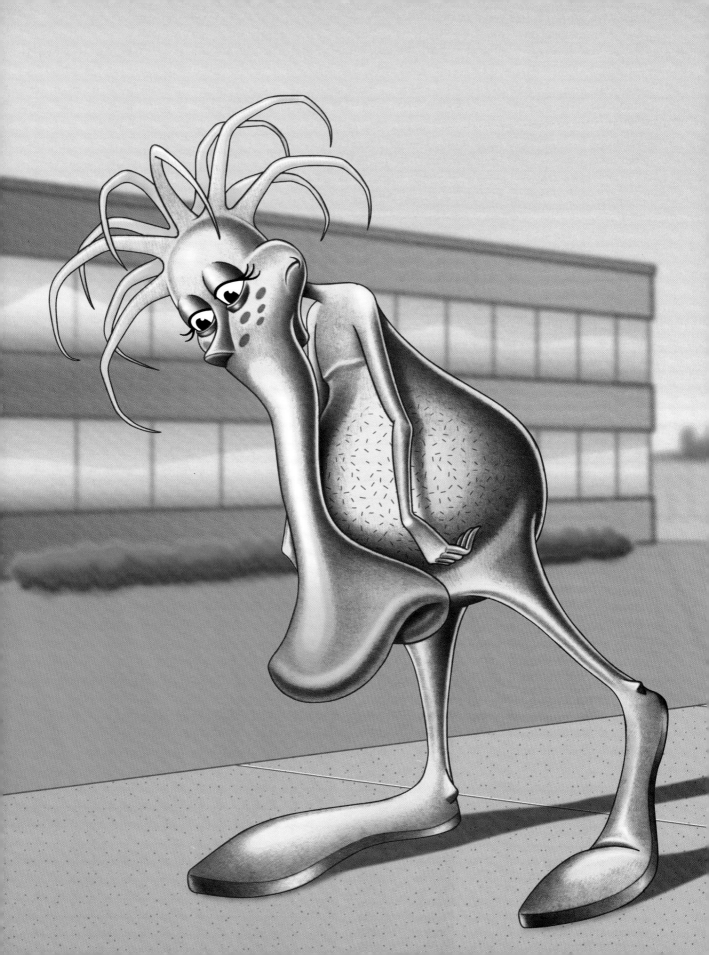

"Oh Snarth, now do you believe me?" cried Katrina. "I tried to tell you this wouldn't work!" But the Snarth just sobbed noisily. Marcus Wilson and some of the other children came up and patted it gently on the lips.

The bell rang to end recess. Katrina and the other children sadly waved goodbye as the Snarth went slinking off toward home, head down and lips low. Poor old Snarth! But at least it had one day in school.

That night at the dinner table, Katrina's mom was about to ask her usual questions about school. But Katrina caught her mother's eye and shook her head, motioning toward the Snarth. Instead Mrs. Mann turned to the Snarth and said brightly, "Who wants another corn dog?"

"Not me, thank you," said the Snarth in a toneless voice, and then fell silent for the rest of the meal. It didn't even so much as chuckle when Mr. Mann got a violent case of the hiccups a few minutes later.

The next day, Katrina's science class was covering her favorite subject, the dinosaurs. Mrs. Callahan showed the class some pictures of different kinds of dinosaurs.

"The brachiosaurus was one of the largest dinosaurs," she said, holding up the biggest picture. "It weighed 70 tons, was 70 feet long and stood 40 feet tall."

"Beep! I knew one that was bigger than that!" squeaked a wet, lippy voice from the back of the room. Without turning around, Katrina covered her face with her hands.

"Zora was my best dinosaur friend," continued the voice, which of course belonged to the Snarth. "She was very big and very beautiful. She had wings like a dragon, a neck like a giraffe and a big, fat stomach!" The Snarth giggled, and some of the children started laughing, too.

Mrs. Callahan stared at the Snarth. "What do you mean, your 'dinosaur friend?'" she demanded. "The dinosaurs lived hundreds of millions of years ago."

"That's true," said the Snarth, sounding a little sad. "Even though Zora died 196,263,891-and-a-half years ago, I remember her like it was yesterday."

Katrina could no longer remain silent. "It doesn't mean any disrespect, Mrs. Callahan," she called out. "The Snarth really has lived for millions of years, and I'm sure it really did know some dinosaurs personally. And now if you'll excuse it, it really must be going!"

Katrina grabbed the Snarth, putting a clamp-hold on its lips, and whisked it out into the hall—where they collided head-on with Mr. Flatt.

Mr. Flatt's face turned bright pink. Then it turned red. It was about to turn purple when he exploded.

"I thought I told you to keep this slimy-lipped creature away from here!" he roared. The Snarth cowered next to Katrina.

But Katrina stood very tall, summoned up all her courage, and said,
"If you please, Sir, why can't the Snarth come to school with me? It knows
a lot already, especially about hist—"

"I'll tell you why!" bellowed Mr. Flatt.

"To come to school you have to be one of three things: A, a child. B, a grown-up. C, an animal." Katrina was puzzled for a moment, but then remembered the hamsters in the second grade classroom. "And that—" he continued, pointing a stubby finger down at the quivering Snarth—"is clearly none of the above. It does not belong here!"

"And if I ever see it here again, I'm going to call the police, the FBI, and the SPCA!" With that he turned on his heel and waddled briskly down the hall.

It wasn't so much the police or the FBI that worried Katrina, it was the SPCA. A neighbor had called them one time about the Snarth, and it had taken forever to get things straightened out. But most of all, Katrina couldn't figure out why Mr. Flatt was so mean to a creature as harmless as the Snarth. What was wrong with wanting to have fun and make people happy?

As frightened as it had seemed to be that day with Mr. Flatt, the Snarth just couldn't stay away from Cedarville Elementary. Katrina didn't actually see it there for several weeks, but the evidence was everywhere. She heard the kids on the school bus asking each other about the strange things that were going on when no one was around. Who had left a beautiful speckled pebble in the pocket of each pupil's coat? Who had decorated the library with bright red berries and yellow maple leaves? How had tiny baskets filled with violet blossoms found their way onto all the teachers' desks? Of course Katrina knew who was responsible, but she didn't say anything. She knew it was only a matter of time before the Snarth would show its face again.

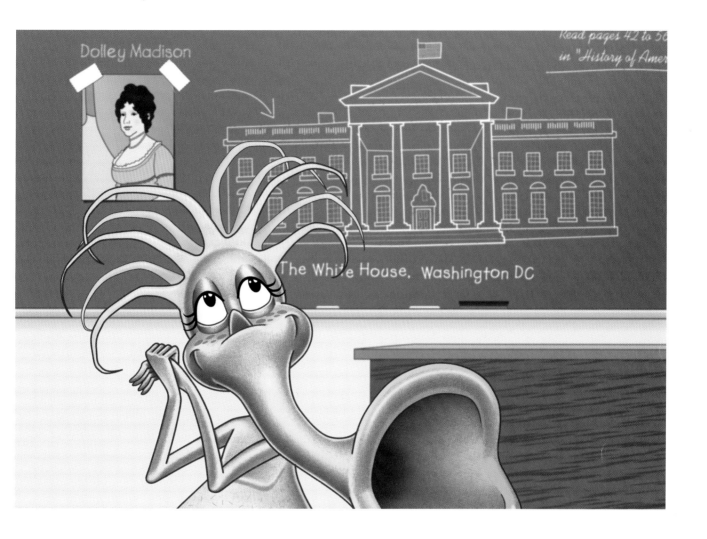

Sure enough, one morning Katrina walked into her classroom to find the Snarth sitting smack in the middle of a circle of children, telling stories about people it had known long ago. Katrina saw Mrs. Callahan pulling the Snarth aside, and the very next day she announced something new: History Hour with the Snarth. Every day before lunch, Katrina and her classmates listened as the high-pitched voice made the past come alive. Katrina learned, to her surprise, that the Snarth had helped Dolley Madison pick out the first White House china! Also, it seemed that Galileo got the idea for the tele-scope from seeing the Snarth's lips in action. Sometimes it seemed as though the Snarth had known everyone in history, but of course that was impossi-ble. "I never met Marie Antoinette," it confessed, "but I loved her hair-do!"

While the children were learning history from the Snarth, the Snarth was learning how to stay one step ahead of Mr. Flatt. It listened and watched so hard that Katrina could almost see its lips quivering like an antenna. At the first sound of those heavy, angry footsteps, the Snarth would suck itself into the heating vents before Mr. Flatt could turn the corner. Or it would spot his flat-headed silhouette through a frosted glass window, and dive lips-first under Mrs. Callahan's desk.

One day, Mr. Flatt opened the door too fast for the Snarth to escape. Katrina quickly stuck out her lips and the other children imitated her, creating a camouflaging sea of Snarth-like faces. Presented with such a revolting spectacle, Mr. Flatt snarled and stalked out.

For a while after that, everything was fine. Katrina wasn't nervous about school anymore. She knew everyone now and had made plenty of friends, thanks in part to the Snarth's popularity. She certainly didn't have to avoid talking about school at the dinner table, either. In fact, the Snarth was the one who talked non-stop about school, its eyes shining and its lips vibrating with excitement. Katrina had to smile to see the Snarth so happy, but all the same she didn't believe it could avoid Mr. Flatt forever. At the back of her mind lived a nagging thought: Something bad is bound to happen.

And, of course, it did. It happened on a day when the Snarth was having too much fun to watch and listen for Mr. Flatt. The children in Katrina's class were learning gymnastics. The Snarth was right in the middle of everything, laughing and singing as it tumbled on the mats, spun around the bars, and danced along the balance beam on its long, flat feet. It tickled Katrina until she nearly fell off the still rings. It laughed like a cross between a hyena and a screech owl. All the kids laughed and clapped as the Snarth began flying higher and higher on the trampoline, bouncing on its lips and turning fancy somersaults in the air.

And then it happened…

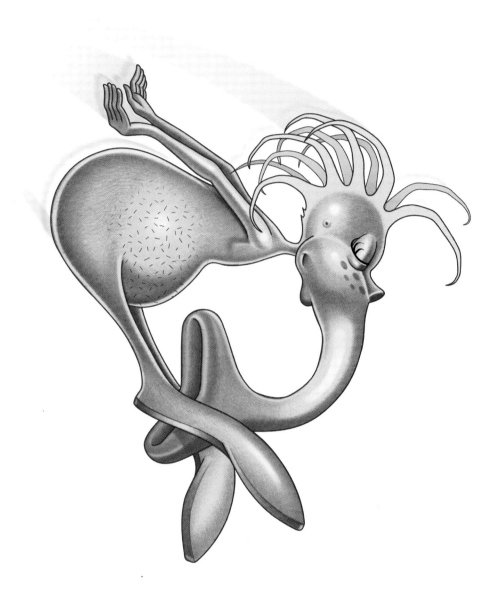

The Snarth turned over and over in the air and landed—SPLATT!—right on top of Mr. Flatt's head.

Mr. Flatt had lots of different ways of getting mad. This time he didn't turn red, and he didn't yell. He was very quiet, and his face was as hard as a stone. He didn't move except to clamp his fists around the Snarth's ankles, which were dangling right below his ears.

Katrina and her classmates watched frozen as Mr. Flatt marched out of the gym with the Snarth, its eyes like saucers, perched on the flat top of his head. Katrina ran after them, but the heavy gym door slammed in her face. Two seconds later, it flew open and Mr. Flatt grabbed Katrina's hand. "You come too, young lady. You're in a lot of trouble!" snarled Mr. Flatt as he stomped down the hall. He moved so fast that Katrina's feet practically left the ground.

Mr. Flatt had a big, dark office with a big, dark desk and a small, pale secretary sitting out front. As he rushed past her he snapped, "Get Katrina Mann's parents on the phone, Miss Gray. And call the SPCA, too!" Miss Gray, who had received a lovely seashell from the Snarth just the week before, watched sadly as Mr. Flatt, Katrina and the Snarth disappeared into the inner office. The door closed behind them.

Mr. Flatt pushed Katrina into a chair. Then he leaned over and dumped the Snarth off of his head, onto the floor. The Snarth looked up beseechingly at Mr. Flatt. "Please," it cried, "don't bother Mr. and Mrs. Mann. They've been so good to me. I'll do whatever you say!"

Katrina's eyes filled with tears. Then she saw a strange sight: Mr. Flatt's teeth. He actually smiled. He had won. He opened his office door and said, "Cancel those calls, Miss Gray. I think everything's going to be fine now."

Turning back to the Snarth he said, "I want your word that you'll never again try to go where you don't belong." But the Snarth wasn't listening—it was gazing at a picture on Mr. Flatt's big, dark wall.

"I knew him!" cried the Snarth, pointing up to the picture of the tall man wearing a stovepipe hat. "He was one of the best humans I ever knew. I used to polish his shoes by flubbering them!"

"What?!" sputtered Mr. Flatt. "What would YOU know about Abraham Lincoln?"

"Well," said the Snarth, "I know some people said he was kind of funny looking. They laughed at him because of the way he looked and the way he acted. But he didn't care, because he just wanted to help people and make things better for them."

Katrina thought she actually saw Mr. Flatt wince! What was he thinking? Maybe he was remembering being laughed at when he was in school. Looking at him now, Katrina could easily imagine that other kids would tease him for being short and chubby and having a flat head. Maybe that was what had made him so mean.

The Snarth was still staring at that picture on the wall. "And you know what else?" it continued. "People stopped laughing at Mr. Lincoln because he tried to help everybody just the same. He kept doing what he knew was right."

Katrina held her breath as she watched Mr. Flatt looking intently at the Snarth. He was very quiet and the snarl on his face was beginning to fade.

The Snarth turned its head and looked directly at Mr. Flatt. Their eyes met. "Mr. Lincoln worked very hard to bring people together even when they didn't get along," it said softly. "He thought everybody should be treated right, no matter what they looked like or anything else about them."

Mr. Flatt turned his gaze to the picture on the wall. "Yes," he said under his breath, " 'With malice toward none…with charity toward all.' "

There was a long moment of silence. All Katrina could hear was the clock ticking and her own heart pounding. Suddenly Mr. Flatt turned to the Snarth.

"Snarth, I think you've taught me a lesson today. You and your old friend, Mr. Lincoln. You may keep coming to my school just as long as you like."

"YIPPEE!" screamed the Snarth. It leaped into the air, planted a big wet kiss on the top of Mr. Flatt's head, and grabbed Katrina's hands, whirling her around in a quick dance. Then it tore out of the room, leaving a faint trail of excited screeching. Katrina thought Mr. Flatt looked for just a moment as though he regretted his decision. But then he smiled at her, this time without showing his teeth.

Miss Gray peeked into the office. "Should I attempt to retrieve and detain the—uh, creature, Sir?" she asked.

"No, there's no need for that, Miss Gray," replied Mr. Flatt. "That creature is a new pupil in our school."

That evening, Mrs. Mann cooked the Snarth's favorite dinner of corn dogs with peanut butter sauce. There were candles on the table and a powdered doughnut pie for dessert.

After the dishes were cleared, Mrs. Mann handed the Snarth a big box with a fancy purple ribbon around it. "This is from all of us, sweetie."

Katrina and her parents gathered around the Snarth as it opened the box. Everyone was beaming. The Snarth's lips glistened in the candlelight.

In the box was a pass to get on the school bus...and the most beautiful lunch box the Snarth had ever seen. Orange plaid, purple polka dots and neon yellow squiggles all jumbled together!